FOR
AMIE,
my big sis

COURTESY
INTEGRITY
PERSEVERANCE
SELF-CONTROL
INDOMITABLE SPIRIT

TAE KWON DO
Promotion Test
SATURDAY 1PM
Families & Friends
ARE WELCOME

Library of Congress Cataloging-in-Publication Data

Names: Kim, Aram, author, illustrator. | Title: Let's go to taekwondo: a story about persistence,
bravery, and breaking boards / Aram Kim. | Description: New York : Holiday House, [2020]
Summary: Yoomi loves studying taekwondo and wants to earn a yellow belt, but she is afraid
to break a board until Grandma comes to the rescue. Includes facts about taekwondo and glossary
of basic Korean terms. | Identifiers: LCCN 2019014339 | ISBN 9780823443604 (hardcover)
Subjects: LCSH: Tae kwon do—Fiction. | Perseverance (Ethics)—Fiction.
Grandmothers—Fiction. | Korean Americans—Fiction.
Classification: LCC PZ7.1.K55 Let 2020 | DDC [E]—dc23
LC record available at https://lccn.loc.gov/2019014339

LET'S GO TO TAEKWONDO!

A STORY ABOUT PERSISTENCE, BRAVERY, AND BREAKING BOARDS

ARAM KIM

HOLIDAY HOUSE NEW YORK

Grandma takes Yoomi to the dojang today.

Her brothers Jun and Yoon are already there.

Yoomi bows as she enters the room.

Then she bows to Master Cho . . .

and her classmates—Gaby, Ravi, and Alejandra.

First, Yoomi and her friends meditate.

Then they run and jump.

Older kids help them with their forms.

They count their kicks in Korean.
"Hana, dul, set, net."

Yoomi and her friends are getting ready
to take the test for their yellow belts.

But when it's time to
break the board . . .

But when it's time to
break the board . . .

Master Cho brings out boards.
"Yay!" says Alejandra.

Everyone looks at Yoomi.

Yoomi looks at the board.

The more she looks,

the bigger it seems to get.

"Don't think about hitting the board,"
Master Cho says. "Try reaching through."

But Yoomi is just thinking about hurting her hand.

"It's not about strength," says Master Cho.
"It's about focus."

Yoomi tries to focus. She reaches out. . . .

But at the last moment, Yoomi pulls back.

"Don't worry," says Master Cho. "You can try again tomorrow."

The next day, a new student joins the class.
His name is Caleb. Master Cho asks Yoomi to
help him.

Yoomi shows Caleb how
to bow and show respect.

Yoomi and her friends show how they kick
and punch.

That night, Yoomi can't sleep.

The next day, Yoomi tells Grandma, "I'm not feeling well and I can't go to dojang."

"Okay," Grandma says.

The day after that, she tells Grandma,
"I have too much homework so I can't go to dojang."

"Okay," Grandma says.

The next day, Yoomi tells Grandma,

"I'M QUITTING TAEKWONDO!!!"

"Okay," Grandma says.

Yoomi was startled to hear Grandma shout.
"I want to call my sister, Misook, in Korea, but
I just can't do it!"

"Just keep trying, Grandma,"
Yoomi says. "You'll figure it out."

"Yes, I will," Grandma
says.

"I'll try this . . .
and this. . . . No."

"I'll try this . . .
and this . . ."

"Misook, it's you!
Annyeong! Hello!"

"I will keep trying, too."

Yoomi breathes deeply and focuses.

She imagines a board.

"Hana, dul," she whispers.

set!

Yoomi slashes through the imaginary board,

through grandma's favorite rice crackers,

and almost through the paper towel roll!

The next day, Yoomi changes into her dobok.
"I'm ready," she tells Grandma.

At the dojang, everyone is waiting.

Yoomi demonstrates her punches

and kicks.

"Are you ready?" Master Cho asks.

Yoomi's heart pounds. She breathes . . . and then . . .

Everyone cheers.

Especially Grandma.

1. 태권도 TAEKWONDO [TEH-KWAHN-DOH]

Taekwondo is the art of self-defense that originated in Korea. It teaches not only physical fighting skills, but also ways of enhancing our spirits and our lives through training the body and the mind. Five tenets of taekwondo are courtesy, integrity, perseverance, self-control, and indomitable spirit. Taekwondo is practiced by all age groups in more than 190 countries worldwide and is an official sport in the Olympic games.

2. 태극기 TAEGEUKGI [TEH-GUH-KEE]

Taegeukgi is the national flag of South Korea. Taekwondo dojangs display Taegeukgi along with one's own country's national flag as a sign of respect for the country where taekwondo originated.

3. 오방색 OBANGSEK [OH-BAHNG-SEK]

The most basic colors of taekwondo belts are white, yellow, blue, red, and black. These colors are called obangsek, the five cardinal colors of Korean tradition. Each color represents an important natural element, and together they create harmony. WHITE symbolizes metal and west. YELLOW symbolizes earth and center. BLUE symbolizes wood and east. RED symbolizes fire and south. BLACK symbolizes water and north.

These five cardinal colors are found throughout Korean culture, including patterns, traditional clothes, food, and more.

Today, many dojangs have adopted more colors such as green, purple, and brown to encourage students to achieve higher goals.

4. KOREAN WORDS

Basic terms and commands used in taekwondo are in Korean. A few basic words include:

도장 DOJANG [DOH-JAHNG]: training hall

도복 DOBOK [DOH-BOHK]: uniform

차렷 CHARYUT [CHAHR-YUHT]: attention

준비 JOONBI [JOON-BEE]: ready

시작 SIJAK [SHEE-JAHK]: begin

Pronunciation of the Korean words (in brackets) has been adapted for speakers of American English.

Visit aramkim.com to hear the author pronounce the Korean words.

Counting one to ten in Korean:

1	하나	HANA [HAH-NAH]
2	둘	DUL [DOOL]
3	셋	SET [SEHT]
4	넷	NET [NEHT]
5	다섯	DASEOT [DAH-SUHT]
6	여섯	YEOSEOT [YUHSS-UHT]
7	일곱	IL-GOP [IL-GOHP]
8	여덟	YEODUL [YUHD-UHLL]
9	아홉	AH-HOP [AH-HOHP]
10	열	YEOL [YUHL]

WHITE

YELLOW

CALEB 캐일럽

GABY 개비

ALEJANDRA 알레한드라

RAVI 라비

YOOMI 유미

OCT 2 0 REC'D